RIVERSIDE CO EM

S0-CBQ-304

RIVERSIDE COUNTY LIBRARY SYSTEM

# MY FIRST AIRPLANE RIDE

## BY PATRICIA HUBBELL
## ILLUSTRATED BY NANCY SPEIR

Marshall Cavendish Children

Text copyright © 2008 by Patricia Hubbell
Illustrations copyright © 2008 by Nancy Speir

All rights reserved
Marshall Cavendish Corporation, 99 White Plains Road, Tarrytown, NY 10591
www.marshallcavendish.us/kids

Hubbell, Patricia.
My first airplane ride / by Patricia Hubbell ; [Nancy Speir, illustrator]. — 1st ed.
p. cm.
Summary: Follows a young traveler through a first airplane ride, from takeoff to touchdown.
ISBN 978-0-7614-5436-6
[1. Stories in rhyme. 2. Air travel—Fiction.] I. Speir, Nancy, ill. II. Title.
PZ8.3.H848My 2008
[E]—dc22
2007041979

The illustrations are rendered in acrylic paint on illustration board.
Book design by Becky Terhune
Editor: Margery Cuyler

Printed in Malaysia
First edition
1 3 5 6 4 2

 Marshall Cavendish
Children

FOR SHOSHI, SHIRA, MEGAN—

THREE VETERAN TRAVELERS!

—P.H.

FOR RALPH

—N.S.

Grandma says, "Come visit me!"

Time to go! Lots to see!

Airport ahead. We park our car.

Plane will take us far, far, far!

Go inside for our boarding pass.

Watch the planes through the big plate glass.

Security check. Take off each shoe.

Lift our suitcases. Backpacks, too.

Read the signs. Find our gate.

Play. Talk. Laugh. Wait.

Walk the Jetway. Time to fly!

Soon our plane will be so high!

Aisles. Seats. Luggage rack.

There's a bathroom in the back.

Look around. Find our seats.

Snuggle down. Have some treats.

Attendant tells us what to do.

She's part of the busy crew.

Flying time is almost here.

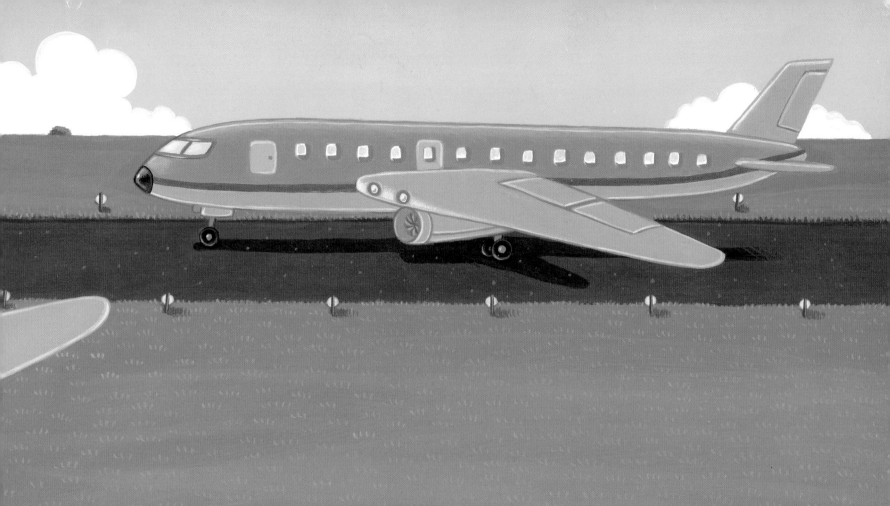

We'll take off when the runway's clear.

Air controller says, "Okay!"

Plane taxis. We're on our way!

**LIFTING!** Whooshing! **CRUISING!** Soaring!

**SHUDDERING!** Shaking! **RUMBLING!** Roaring!

Watch a movie. Read a book.

Out the window—Look! Look!

Forest. Lake. Highway. Town.

Earth's so small as we look down.

Here's a pillow. Time for naps.

Teddy bears snooze on our laps.

Snacks are coming on a tray.

What a long, exciting day!

Time to land. Airport below!

Wheels touch down. Get set. . . . Let's go!

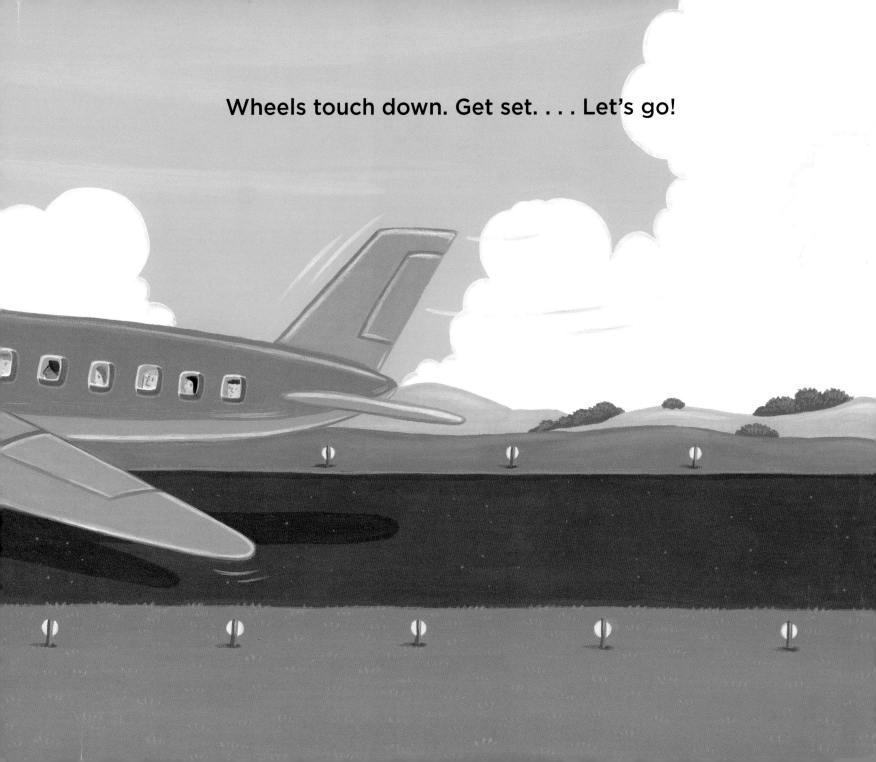

Back through the Jetway. Hurry! Ohhh . . .

Grandma's waving! Hug hello!